D1445399

WISE UP, SILLY OWL!

Dedication:

To Loretta, Nancy, and Julia
—S.M.

About Hans Wilhelm:

Hans Wilhelm is one of America's foremost author/illustrators for children's books with over
35 million books in print. He has created over 200 books many of which have won international awards
and prizes. Other Wilhelm books published by Barron's are *The Book of Courage, Patches' Easter
Adventure, Friends Around the World,* and *What Are Friends For?*

He and his artist wife Judy Henderson live in Weston, CT. For more info: www.hanswilhelm.com

About Steve Metzger:

Steve Metzger has written many books for young children, including *The Dinofours* series
(illustrated by Hans Wilhelm), *The Falling Leaves, The Great Turkey Race,* and *The Mixed-Up
Alphabet.* He lives in NYC with his wife and daughter.

All inquiries should be addressed to:
Barron's Educational Series, Inc.
250 Wireless Boulevard
Hauppauge, NY 11788
www.barronseduc.com

Library of Congress Control Number: 2008927422

ISBN-13: 978-0-7641-6165-0
ISBN-10: 0-7641-6165-2

Printed in China
9 8 7 6 5 4 3 2 1

WISE UP, SILLY OWL!

Steve Metzger

Illustrated by Hans Wilhelm

BARRON'S

It was late afternoon in the great woods when Spotty the owl woke up.

"Wheee!" Spotty yelled as he flew out the window and soared into the sky. He twirled around ten times, landed on a tree, and did a bouncy dance.

All at once, he heard a familiar voice.
"Spotty, it's time for your lesson!" It was
his father, the Wise Old Owl.

I don't want to go home,
Spotty thought. *But I guess I have
to.* He flew through the window
and found his father waiting
for him.

"Let's begin," his father said. "Today's lesson will be 'Birds of a feather flock together.'" As his father lectured, Spotty slid off his chair and stood on his head. Then, he made silly faces.

"Spotty!" Father Owl said angrily. "You're not listening! How are you going to become a wise owl and help the forest animals?"

"But I don't want to be wise!" Spotty answered. "I just want to be silly." His ancestors were horrified.

Just then, a blue jay flew in through the window with a note.

Father Owl turned to Spotty. "Oh dear, I have to help your Aunt Evelyn fix her leaky roof. While I'm away, you're in charge."
Spotty nodded.

"Try to remember some of what I taught you," Father Owl said as he took off. "I should be back tomorrow. Goodbye."

This will be easy, Spotty thought. *I'll just pretend to be wise. Nobody will know I'm not.* His ancestors, watching from the pictures on the wall, weren't so sure.

There was a knock on the door. "Come in," Spotty called out.
"Are *you* the Wise Old Owl?" Susie Squirrel asked.
"No, that's my father," Spotty responded. "He had to go away.
How can I help you?"
"I forgot where I buried my acorns," Susie began. "And it's almost winter."
Spotty tried to look thoughtful. Then he sang:
  "Climb a tree, dance around.
  Run and jump, look on the ground."
"Now you may go," Spotty added. "Goodbye."

Susie scurried off. After a few seconds, Spotty followed her to see what would happen. Susie did exactly as she was told.

After dozens of acorns fell to the ground, she happily gathered them. "That young owl is very wise," she excitedly told her friends and neighbors.

"This wise stuff is a snap!" Spotty said as he flew home.

The next morning, Max Beaver showed up.

"Susie told me you gave her good advice," Max said. "I have a problem, too."

"What is it?" Spotty asked.

"Every time I build a dam, it falls apart," Max explained. "What should I do?"

Spotty smiled wisely and sang:

"*Gather sticks, pile them tall.*
Sit on top and have a ball!"

Again, Spotty followed to see what would happen. But this time Max's dam came apart and he fell into the water...splash! "That young owl is not wise at all," he shouted. "I'm going to tell everyone!"

Spotty's wings drooped as he flew home and crawled into bed. "I really messed up," he said.

Later that afternoon, Rosie Robin flew onto the windowsill and began chirping. "Is the Wise Old Owl back?" she asked. "I have a problem, but I heard you're too silly."

"I can be wise, I know I can," Spotty replied. "Give me a chance."

"Well," Rosie said. "There's a fox near my tree. I'm afraid he'll get my eggs."

Spotty looked at one of his father's signs: Birds of a feather flock together. "I've got it!" Then he sang:

"Call your friends from far and near,
They'll make that mean fox disappear."

"I don't think that will work," Rosie said, "but I've got to try something." As she flew out the window, she yelled, "Help me! Help me!"

This time, Spotty stayed home. He paced back and forth. "I hope everything turns out okay." He looked up at his ancestors. They seemed a little nervous, too.

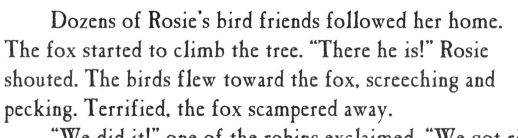

Dozens of Rosie's bird friends followed her home. The fox started to climb the tree. "There he is!" Rosie shouted. The birds flew toward the fox, screeching and pecking. Terrified, the fox scampered away.

"We did it!" one of the robins exclaimed. "We got rid of the fox!"

"Yes!" Rosie said. "Thanks to Spotty's good advice."

The robins flew from burrow to den, spreading the word about Spotty.

A few minutes later, Spotty heard a commotion. He saw a large group of animals coming toward him.

Uh-oh! he thought. *Maybe they're mad at me!*

"Hooray for Spotty!" Rosie chirped. "You saved the day!"

"What!?!" Spotty exclaimed.

"You helped Rosie scare the fox away," Susie Squirrel added. "She told us all about it!"

"Let's have a party for Spotty, the Wise Young Owl!" Rosie said.

"I love parties!" Spotty said with a big smile.

The forest animals were dancing to the music of the Rockin' Rabbits when the Wise Old Owl came home.

"What's going on?" he asked.

"We're having a party!" Rosie said. "Your son's wise words helped me save my eggs from the fox!"

"Hooray for Spotty!" the other animals cheered. Even Max Beaver joined in.

Wise Old Owl put his wing around Spotty and smiled.
"I'm very proud of you." Then, he sang:
"Let's celebrate, it's no surprise.
I have a son who's very wise."